WHISPERS IN THE FOG

E. M. WALLIS

Acknowledgements.

Many thanks to my proof readers, Debbie Rundle and Trudy Wallis, your patience picking out my typos and encouraging feedback are appreciated.

Thank you to the real Rosie Bennetts, who let me use her name.

CONTENTS

Title Page

Copyright

Dedication

Chapter one   2

Chapter two   11

Chapter three   17

Chapter four   30

Chapter five   35

Chapter six   41

Chapter seven   47

Chapter eight   52

Chapter nine   64

E.M.WALLIS

Whispers in the fog

CHAPTER ONE

Lillie cut a spectral silhouette through the faint morning light, with purposeful strides. Navigating the coast path, the mist embraced her like a ghostly shroud as she headed towards the road.

Her pale green eyes flickered with every movement, revealing glimpses of a more mysterious and profound world, one she would rather keep away from.

After moments, she reached the end of the track, slight echoes of whispers danced on the edge of her perception.

Gritting her teeth, she struggled to block out the persistent pleas which toyed with her thoughts, a lingering reminder of the psychic gifts she spent so much time trying to suppress.

With the dense fog bearing down on her like a foreboding threat, Lillie hesitated, a sense of unsettling in her gut.

The delicate silence gave way to the piercing sound of brakes screeching, she sensed the echo reverberating inside her.

In an attempt to chase away the noise, she blinked.

Gripping her head, she gasped, attempting to erase what she knew to be an impending premonition, but it persisted.

The fog parted before her, an unknown force guiding her. In an instant, she found herself carried away, propelled by some unseen energy, to the back of a bus.

The harsh clang of metal striking the vehicle, reached her ears. The bus jolted as it got pushed across the road, by a delivery truck, into the path of oncoming traffic.

Lillie viewed the lorry driver's scared eyes. visible to her through the windscreen, his face reflecting horror. Nothing he did would prevent the unfolding carnage.

"I don't want to watch it. I don't want this," she said, trying to clear her mind. "Go away. Leave me alone."

Terror consumed her at what she could see. A boy no older than five years old. The force of the accident flung the power of the impact ripped him from her.

Despite feeling compelled to intervene, she remained an observer, a mere spirit within her own premonition, rendered helpless. His long, curly blonde locks obscured the damage inflicted by the trauma on his young face.

In a flash, she arrived back on the street, panting for air and trembling. Shaking her head with ferocious power, trying to rid her mind of the images of the crash.

Two teenage boys pushed past her on the pavement.

"Away with the fairies, Mad Lillie Pad, yeah!" One of them said. They both laughed.

Recoiling, she hoped to hide in the returning fog.

"Leave her alone, she's not doing you any harm," said a firm female voice from behind her.

"What are you, her carer?" The other lad said, smirking. They kicked their empty beer cans towards her, before losing interest and disappearing into a side street.

"Are you okay miss?" The woman said, putting a steadying hand on Lillie's arm.

Lillie raised her gaze to the woman, who towered over her. Looking up into her eyes she could see kindness and yet also a sense of something else.

"Yes. I think so. Just a funny turn." She said.

Something tried to flash in her head. A vision. Blinking, she attempted to push it back, not wanting any more trips to the future at that moment.

With a faint, empathetic smile, the woman offered her hand.

"Why don't you sit a while, you are a little shaken," she said.

"Thank you." Lillie said. Taking her arm.

"I'm Rosie and this is Sam. Here let me help you to the bench" she said, offering her hand.

Glancing down, Lillie saw a youngster, perhaps five years old. He held Rosie's hand. Her son she presumed. He shared his mum's kind emerald eyes and shoulder length wavy, blonde hair.

The bus flashed before her eyes again, like a lightning strike. Taken by surprise, she flinched.

The image of the lifeless child now etched in her mind's eye. The colour drained from her face.

"No," she said.

"Sorry?" Rosie said, frowning.

"Nothing" Lillie said. The response tumbled from her lips. As her thoughts scrambled into a whirlwind. Distracted by a desperate search for something to put off their terrible fate.

"The rantings of a mad woman. Mad Lillie Pad," she said, laughing, trying to make light of her comment.

"Really?" Rosie said, for the first time seeming a little unsettled.

"Really nothing, or really a mad woman?" she answered, attempting to laugh again but her nerves distorted it. It sounded more like a cackle.

Rosie became even more alarmed by Lillie's comments and attitude. "Well, if you are okay miss then we must be getting along now, we have a bus to catch," she said.

"You can't get on the bus, wait for a later one," Lillie said, grabbing Rosie's elbow in a sudden panic.

"You're scaring me now," Rosie said, frowning.

She squirmed in an attempt to wrestle her arm free from Lillie's grasp. Each pull a silent struggle etched on her face.

Lillie's eyes darted, showing her nervousness and despair. trying to find the right words to convince Rosie to avoid the impending disaster.

The mist gathered around them, generating a desolate post-apocalyptic scene.

"Please, I get it, it sounds insane, but it will be dangerous to get on the bus. A terrible crash is going to happen...I saw it," she said.

The expression on Rosie's face shifted from concern to scepticism.

"What are you saying? How can you tell? You can't know," she asked

After a hesitation, she continued. "Are you sure you're alright? You appear, so... troubled."

Lillie bit her lip. Grappling with an internal struggle to convey the urgency, she knew she sounded more like a madwoman.

"I have visions. I see things and I saw you and your son, in the middle of a crash," she said.

Frustration and distress grew in her. Reaching out again, she tried to grab Rosie's other arm. Rosie recoiled.

"Please wait," she said. "Take a later one. Now, I can't explain everything. I promise you; I'm not making this up. You are in danger I need you to trust me."

Rosie's eyes widened in disbelief, pulling her elbow away with a sharp motion.

"You see the future? You can't mean it. This is absurd. Please, I have to go to the stop with Sam," she said.

For a brief moment, Lillie protested, but her resistance gave way to the inevitable. An acceptance, with reluctance, of how every tug only deepened the portrait of "Mad Lillie Pad."

Rosie hurried away, dragging her child with her. Turning her head as she went. The deep rumble of the number seven bus getting closer. Picking up pace, she made it to the bus stop in time.

Spinning on her heel, Lillie shot off in the opposite direction. The events of her premonition loomed. A vivid projection she feared witnessing in reality. Guilt gnawed at her, a remorseful echo for not fighting harder to rescue them.

In her retreat, the ill-fated bus Rosie intended to board passed her. A cruel snapshot of the fate she hoped to avoid.

Dropping into a back street, anxious to be away from the

impending crash, she scuttled along the cobbles. Here, the mist hung heavy again, enveloping her as if the road surface and brick facets embraced her within it.

Quiet words drifted through the encompassing soup. Insistent, they scorned her.

A voice, louder than the whispers, slashed through the soft babble. "Sometimes the echoes of destiny can't be silenced; they guide us whether we choose to listen or not."

The haunting phrases echoed in the solitude of Lillie's secluded presence.

Startled and confused, she found herself in a state of surprise. Shivering as a chill went down her spine, her eyes darted toward the sound.

Despite fog veiling much of the cobbled lane, her instincts told her that no one could be there.

The coded message lingered as an unsettling thought. The words burned in her mind. Nodding, she tried to hide her discomfort beneath a calm exterior.

The invisible speaker grew quiet. Leaving Lillie to mull about the disturbing remarks.

Torn between the urge to flee the foggy alley and the intrigue surrounding the voice's mysterious remark, she paused.

The mist clutched her like a phantom's fingers, as though an alien energy resonated in the air itself.

Long breath taken, she endeavoured to drive away the terrifying premonition. It lingered in her thoughts. An enduring stain on her mind.

Inner turmoil and mounting confusion grew, she clenched her fists as they trembled at her sides. Brows furrowed in deep lines; she replayed the vision of the bus crash. A heavyweight threatened to undermine her resolve as it pressed against her chest.

Ignoring the apprehension gnawing at her insides, she straightened her posture, her jaw set with conviction.

With a shaky breath, she took the first step forward. The muttering in the fog intensified, weaving a complex fabric of warnings and intriguing guidance.

Her racing heartbeat rang out in her eardrums. Each footfall like a thunderclap hitting the pavement. The rhythm drove her onward. It propelled her through the fog choked allies.

The air crackled with tension, charged with the electricity of impending doom.

Moving through the gloomy streets, the world blurred around her. The edges of reality melted away into a haze of uncertainty.

Lillie pressed on. Her senses hyperaware of every sound and shadow which flickered in front of her. The surroundings became saturated with the sharp wound of fright, mingling with the metallic taste of desperation on her tongue.

Each step represented a frantic endeavour to outpace the haunting whispers trailing her. A sense of urgency impelled her along the winding lanes, directed by an invisible hand.

With the passing moments, the weight of the task ahead threatened to crush her spirit. Clenching her fists, she refused to falter.

The thought of the consequences of inaction spurred her forward, a fire igniting within her chest. Chasing after the impossible, she ran, with determination, against time itself.

Lillie pushed through, despite the road in front of her being fraught with obstacles. Her courage unwavering even in the face of overwhelming odds.

So, with each step, she drew closer to the high street, her resolve burning brighter with the passing seconds. Her mind set now on defying destiny.

All she could think about was Rosie and Sam, along with the burden of guilt, for not trying harder to help them. It urged her to act. To do anything she could to alter the impending crash

The fog thinned as she reached the outskirts of town. A desolate landscape unveiled itself, as her destination came into view. It reflected the turmoil within her.

The air vibrated with the distant sound of sirens, echoing the tragedy she sought to avert.

The bus from her premonition, already passed its collection point, rumbled up the hill. Her heart missed a beat, Rosie and Sam could not be seen.

The whispers in the fog swirled around her, their urgency heightening. Lillie's horror-filled dark eyes scanned the surroundings for any sign of them. Racing against the unseen currents of destiny. Now, a conviction that defied reason drove her.

Approaching the bus stop. a silent scream escaped her.

Panic seized her, and she called out. "Where are you?!" she said.

Her voice echoed through the desolate streets. The only noise responding, the distant rattling of the bus vanishing in the distance. A cruel reminder of the ticking clock and time slipping away.

The mist swirled in a ghostly dance.

Lillie hurried to the bench where she had last been with them.

Her head hung in shame. An overwhelming sense of loss washed over her. With hands outstretched and a confused expression on her face, she groped at thin air, as if attempting to turn back time. Lowering her arms, she realised the opportunity to save them ceased to exist.

Desperation etched lines on her face as she took in her surroundings, hoping for a glimpse of the mother and son. The whispers in the fog mocked her, their elusive guidance now dwindling to an uncanny silence.

In the emptiness of the fog-laden streets, Lillie grappled with a profound sense of helplessness. The possibility to alter future events ended, leaving her standing alone in the fading mist, haunted by the recollections of a premonition she could not change.

Hunched over, she portrayed an image of a woman aged by the pain of failure. Bewildered, she hobbled back towards the coastal path.

The fog lifted but her visibility did not improve, instead a veil of tears now obscured it. Blind and debilitated by the anguish of her morning, she, at last, reached the sanctuary of her cottage.

On stepping in she double bolted the door. Turning she leant her back against it, before lowering herself to the floor. There she stayed, composing her nerves. Her knees pulled up to her chest, she shook with an inexplicable force.

Now safe in her homely fortress, the shakes subsided, she moved to take a seat in her favourite wing backed chair.

Clutching an emerald cushion in one hand. Breathing in a slow calming way, she ran her fingers over the velvety, forest green, of the chair's arm. Her frown softened as she settled in. Rocking her head back and forth, she tried to relax and clear her thoughts.

The mist had begun stirring something within her. Something she always made a constant effort to keep at arm's length. Some people referred to it as a gift, Lillie could only ever understand it as a curse.

Staring at the spring meadow wallpaper of the tiny lounge, reminded her of the torment which came from her first premonition. Shutting her eyes, she imagined walking bare foot through those fresh meadows, the soft grass comforting on her feet and. The subtle scents of flowers tickling her nose and throat.

Concentrating, she lost herself in the memory, trying like so many times before to work out why she misinterpreted its meaning all those years ago. The usual vivid vision blurred now; the detail appearing hazy, like viewing it on an old VHS film.

The remaining strands of fog receded, a gradual transformation. Lillie stepped out onto the balcony; a steaming mug of coffee cradled in her hands. Each sip brought warmth to her chilled body. It invigorated her senses as she savoured the rich aroma.

Smiling, she took in the view, her eyes widening in delight. With every passing moment, as the fog retreated, the distorted landscape in front of her underwent a remarkable change.

The earlier-obscured picture began to reveal itself, unveiling a watercolour of coastal splendour. Footpaths snaked their way along the rugged cliffs, leading towards the vast expanse of the sea beyond. Here and there, sheep grazed in contentment. Woolly forms blending seamlessly with the beautiful scenery.

Lifting her gaze to the horizon, a sense of awe washed over her. The ocean stretched out ahead of the cliff edge. Before her she beheld a tranquil, aquatic realm. The surface of the water a serene mirror. The sunlight danced upon the swell, casting a mesmerising kaleidoscope of reflections, which shimmered and sparkled with each gentle wave.

Drawing in a deep breath of salty air, she found calm in what she saw. The fog, cleared from her physical surroundings now drifting away from her own thoughts. Doubt crept in, challenging her previous understanding of the morning's events.

At that moment, she experienced a profound connection to the natural world around her, as though she could be part of something greater than herself. The beauty of the scene before her filled her with a sense of peace and contentment, washing away her morning trauma and leaving her heart buoyant with joy. The anxiety and horror of the bus crash ebbed away.

"Just the insane imaginings of Mad Lillie Pad" she said, to a robin who perched itself on the gnarled branches of the willow tree, which cast shade over the balcony and the lawn below it.

Hugging the coffee cup with her hands, she enjoyed its bittersweet aroma. Searching for calm, she began to settle.

A sudden gust of wind whipped out of the porch door, carrying with it an old photo. The picture vanished between the slats of the decking, leaving only its corner revealed.

Poking it, she teased the photograph from the deck. Tears came to her eyes, as she recognised the person in it, her sister. Her expression fell, the faint smile gone, she closed her eyes and let out a gradual and deliberate sigh.

CHAPTER TWO

Yesterday's nightmare now buried in her mind, Lillie went about her morning ritual with a trained detachment, her steps slow and methodical.

Her home and haven, a quaint Victorian railway cottage, nestled centre of the east and west sidings of the town's long-derelict shunting depot. It could only be accessed by a private footpath which joined the south coast trail, which in turn led to Misthaven's only inbound road.

In the loneliness of her homely retreat, she found solace. A refuge carved out for herself, over the years, in the aftermath of her sister's tragic demise at the meadow lake.

At home she could evade the judgmental comments and intrusive glares of those who scorned her abilities. Here she remained free from those who blamed her for not saving her sister and the others who accused her of a mysterious involvement.

This haven became a place where she wielded control over the incessant waves of whispers, which swept in with the mist. Another accompaniment to her psychic gift, which she could never decipher. The voices which once replayed in her mind were drowned out by the sounds of nature. Such as rustling leaves and the ocean crashing on the shore.

Over the decades, as people moved on and their homes were taken over by newcomer's people forgot the events that took her sister's life, in the scorching sun of the summer of eighty-six.

The name calling of 'Mad Lillie Pad,' however, lived on in people's prejudice of the 'wily,' old recluse that lives in the railway sidings.

Lillie's morning routine became shattered by the monotone of fog horns. Staring out to sea, she stood, her chest tightening with anxiety. The fog rolled closer, a tidal wave of water vapour swallowing the cliff's edge in seconds. It created another world. One that whispered to her.

The fog advanced, enshrouding the path and veiling the cottage, terror took hold of Lillie. Always her visceral response to ward off the encroaching whispers, she hurried around the room closing the blinds. Eager as ever to protect herself from the invisible, but oppressive spectres. Panic fluttered within her.

In the dimness cast by the closed shutters, she surrendered to the haunting embrace. The atmosphere, laden with otherworldly gloom, intensified the memories of the premonition from the day before. The walls were festooned with silhouettes. An unsettling vibration erupted in the silence, mirroring the tumult from inside her.

The blinds, on this occasion, were not enough. Shuddering as the first whispers flowed through the misty air, she picked up her earphones, tuned in to Classic FM on her mobile and slumped into her chair. Squeezing her eyelids shut, she rocked herself to the gentle melody of Tchaikovsky's Symphony No. 6.

Finding comfort in the melancholic music. Despite trying to fight it, the pressure of exhaustion overwhelmed her, and she fell into a troubled sleep.

In the eerie gloom behind the blinds of her living room, her dreams sank to the dark premonition of the day before.

Standing at the intersection, of the coast road and the high street, she waited, holding her breath. With sadness, she stood, a mere spectral visitor unable to intervene, as a supermarket lorry thundered out of the fog.

The vehicle collided with the back end of a bus. It knocked it over, putting it in a spin. It came to a thunderous stop when it hit a shop front. Terrified early morning shoppers scattered from its path.

The emergency services arrived. Police, fire, and paramedic staff all helping to evacuate wounded victims from the crash site. Rosie struggled with a police officer trying to return to the scene of the accident.

Lillie witnessed the sight of firefighters bringing a boy's lifeless body from the wreckage, tears streamed down Rosie's face, as she screamed. Lillie averted her stare and covered her ears.

The soft, dancing classical music changed to the shrill, pulsating rhythm of Lillie's ringtone. Waking with a start, unaccustomed to it ringing, save for the occasional health professional, she stared at the phone in bewilderment. Her heart thumping - she pressed the answer button.

"Eh, hello," she said.

Unaware of the duration of her sleep, she stood and peeked through the blinds to assess the time of day. The absence of fog revealed the sun beginning its descent toward the west.

"Lillie love, Aunt Helena. How are you my dear?" Aunt Helena said. Her air of uplifting enthusiasm familiar to Lillie.

"Oh, aunt, sorry. I hope you haven't been waiting long for me to respond?" Lillie said. "I dozed off in my chair. My age is catching up with me, I suppose."

Aunt Helena, Lillie's sole living relative, possessed an uncanny knack of reaching out to her, at the precise moment, when she needed the encouragement of a friendly voice.

"You've only fifty, spring chicken I say. What nonsense. Is there something going on," she said.

Aunt Helena remained consistent in her approach, direct while never passing judgment on Lillie, in the way the rest of the world did. Lillie regarded her as a connection to sanity and cherished her for it.

"No, I'm a little tired. I think I'm coming down with something," Lillie said, unconvincingly. "I've had a long week."

"Lillie!" she said, sounding as if she was ready to challenge Lillie's protest. "The paper ran a story about the Beaumont family reopening Misthaven Island as a, wait what does it say, 'an ultimate, intimate retreat.' I thought I would come down for a few days and we could sail out for some downtime and a catch-up, it has been ages."

"I remember something a while back about him inheriting the place. I don't know about going out there though. You know, I'm not that sociable. I Like my own company," she said. The thought of having to share a house with people, to socialise and to talk to them about her life made Lillie shudder. "Thank you for asking."

"Come on Lillie you're not a recluse. I thought this would be right up your street. An isolated retreat, no mobile phone signal, no internet," she said.

"I know you find it awkward around people but there are only three other guests," she continued. "They will probably be twitchers, more interested in trying to spot some rare bird than mixing with us. Tell me, please, that you are at least intrigued."

"Well, a little," she said. "You're wrong though. I am a bit off a recluse."

The isolation and lack of online distractions tempted her.

"Just think we will be the first people on the island for decades. How exciting," Aunt Helena said, giggling. " Do you remember when the place used to be open to the public? It must have been years ago."

"Of course, Aunty. I visited it in my childhood. The Beaumont estate held such magic back then," she said. "For me, as a youngster it was an adventure to a far-off land. It happens to only be a few miles off the coast. I can see it on a bright day."

"It's a shame things changed after that tragic accident in the late eighties. The eldest son, I think. Do you recall?"

"Yes, I'm a bit vague on the details now," Lillie answered. "At the time the family issued a heart-breaking statement. I remember they asked for privacy to grieve. They dropped out of the spotlight after that. He was only eighteen, I think. They went through a lot."

"I heard they stopped allowing visitors after that. Is that true Lillie?" Aunt Helena said.

"I think so. Sure, it's been years since anyone was allowed

there. Rumours started spreading, at the time, that they turned the estate into a shrine for their son's memory." Lillie said, shuddering at the thought, the earlier enthusiasm now waning.

"I say? How intriguing. Do you think they still keep it that way?"

"I doubt it. I don't know if it is even the truth, I don't remember all the facts," Lillie said. Trying to cast her mind back.

"No, it was a long time ago." Aunt Helena said.

"Some used to say the rooms are frozen in time, filled with memories of their son. It's become a true mystery over the years. I wouldn't worry about tit though. People mock what they don't understand." She said. Finding it difficult to recall what was fact and what was hearsay.

"I do know it was all about the same time that Jess had her accident. It was horrible the cruel things that people used to say about that. About me. Not everything you come across can be relied upon as the truth."

"Yes, it was hard times, but you got over it. I'm sure the Beaumonts did too," Aunt Helena said. "Speaking of the Beaumont's you know it is all owned by the youngest son now, Miles?"

"Oh, of course, I knew that. I saw it online," Lillie said.

"It appears the inheritance tax caused him a problem. He was forced to sell the mainland house and move to the island. Can you believe it?" said Aunt Helena.

"That's why he's offering the location as a retreat, I guess," answered Lilli.

"Can you imagine? From a family estate to a public holiday destination. What?"

"It must have been a difficult decision for him. I would find it impossible to contemplate losing such a beautiful place."

"Life surprises us sometimes, doesn't it? I wonder if it still holds the same charm, even with the changes. Oh, do say you will come darling."

"I'll think about it. You have sold it to me a bit."

"You make sure you do. We all need somewhere to recharge

our batteries every now and again. By the way, did you know about that bus crash up your way. Awful thing, that poor boy's mother."

Her aunt's words came like a punch to her stomach by a heavyweight boxer. Gasping for air, she leant forward to retch.

"Sweetheart, are you still there?" said Aunt Helena

Lillie ended the call. Still finding it a struggle to breathe, she fumbled with the phone. With her hand shaking she texted Aunty Helena – 'sorry, you know how the signal is here. I'll think about the island trip.' Her hands recoiled, as if scorched, and she released the phone, like she was dropping a hot poker.

Restless, she turned to her habitual calming technique, a constant twisting and releasing of the ends of her hair.

The notion of a secluded sanctuary shielded from the town's critical gaze tugged at her mind. Despite the appeal, a part of her still had a nagging unease about it.

Walking to the bay window, her fingers traced the corners of the blinds. Snapping them open, she blinked. Gazing in the direction of Misthaven Island, she shut her eyes and tried to summon the memories of the picturesque place.

In her mind's eye she saw the quaint manor house with its colourful shutters. The distant hum of the tide lapped the shore and the pleasant aroma of sea salt whiffed by.

A wince sculpted lines in her forehead, the side of her mouth turning down. A sudden, brief wave of tears followed each other down her cheeks. The thought of leaving her haven and source of solace scared her, despite the recent occurrences.

Every tear carried with it memories, cherished moments spent in her secluded cottage and along the twisting coastal paths. The house embodied more than a home; it constituted a tapestry woven with feelings of safety and belonging, sheltered from external influences.

CHAPTER THREE

Rising to a chorus of chaffinches, Lillie swept opened the bedroom curtains. The sun blazed through the window. With no fog to see, Lillie let out a short sigh of relief.

Her pulse quickened as she turned away from the window. Somehow, she now stood on the precipice of a cliff. Below, the tempestuous sea roared. Waves murmured secrets. The fog was back. Whispers echoed from it. They incited a sense of dread in her.

Understanding this to be another vision, and realising it arrived too late for her to act, she balled her hands.

An otherworldly energy pulsed in the air. It infused her surroundings with an unsettling aura. Her steps became uncertain, hesitant, deliberate. Unseen power guided her forward.

A haunting scene unfolded at the side of the clifftop. A surge of disbelief gripped her, causing her breath to hitch in her throat.

A figure, near to not being visible in the tumultuous mist, stood at the edge. It was a young man, dressed in a pinstripe suit. His fingers were outstretched towards the roaring sea below.

The thundering surf echoed with distant cries. They merged with the uncanny whispers that carried through the air. From the depths emerged a spectral hand. Translucent and floating it reached for something unseen.

The man turned to face her. With dismay, she saw a noose around his neck. His vacant eyes met hers. They were filled with an unsettling blend of despair and longing.

A wave of horror gripped her, freezing her in place. The scene etched itself into her consciousness. The menacing manifestation sent a chilling tremor through her.

In a reflex response, she extended a trembling hand toward the ethereal silhouette. Freeing herself from the petrified hold, she took a hesitant step forward. Before she could take another, the setting morphed.

The sights on the clifftop lingering in the recesses of her mind, she now stood in Misthaven Bakery. The warm embrace of fresh baked bread permeated the air, intertwined with the faint hint of acrid burning wood, creating an inviting yet rustic atmosphere.

The clatter of the store triggered sudden visions of shattered glass. In the midst of the bakery's sensory fusion, a new phenomenon seized her. The rhythmic clinking of utensils took on a disconcerting element.

In the flickering glow of the oven, shadows danced on the ceiling. They cast a strange ambiance over the place.

Lillie's senses heightened. Her skin prickling with an inexplicable unease. The air around her had thickened with an unearthly presence, making her shudder.

Without a word spoken, her anxiety grew, her instincts urging her to trust the primal signals her body was sending. A bead of sweat trickle down her back, as she braced herself for the unknown danger that permeated the bakery, ready to face whatever lay ahead.

Her heart raced. Her breath quickened. Her lungs struggled to take in enough oxygen.

An oppressive sense of unexplained nervousness settled over her like a suffocating quilt. Its weight pressed down on her shoulders, leaving her to feel trapped in a world of impending darkness.

The shop's aura appeared to whisper of encroaching gloom.

Her skin prickled with goose bumps as she stood frozen in place. Dropping her head, she held it in her hands. Her mind a whirlwind of confusion. The familiar vines of panic tightened around her chest.

Her legs trembled, threatening to give way. Staggering, her body trembling, she reached out. In a desperate attempt to maintain her balance, she clutched the counter.

"What do you want, who, who's there. Why am I here?" she said, as she backed away. The words close to not being audible above the pounding of her own heart. Each syllable hung heavy in the air, filled with desperation.

A door slammed shut from somewhere out of view. Lillie's pulse quickened at the unexpected noise.

A blood-curdling scream followed, slicing through the atmosphere like a knife. It shocked Lillie to her core.

In an intense reaction, she turned away. Attempting to flee from the source of the terrifying sound, she tried to move her feet. To her horror, they remained rooted to the spot. An anchor held her there, projected by some invisible force. Trapped, ensnared in the unsettling silence that lingered in the wake of the cry.

Her mind raced with a thousand unanswered questions; her heart pounded with a fear unlike any she had ever known.

The spectral hand reappeared. It began to solidify into a full - bodied ghostly figure. Transfixed she stood as more ethereal beings started emerging from different corners of the bakery. Each one circled by a haze of smoke. An intense gaze, from them, locked on her.

Even with the heat, she shivered, as their changing forms surrounded her. The ghoulish presence began to suffocate her.

From nowhere, a blinding light flooded through the windows. Within the brilliance, she caught a glimpse of her late sister's face flickering. It left her with a beacon of hope amidst the encroaching despair.

Newfound resolve coursed through her veins. Stepping forward, her determination became unyielding in the face of the supernatural onslaught.

Approaching the illumination, a sudden searing stench assaulted her nostrils, causing her to gag as burns began to appear on the skin of each apparition.

The glow intensified, its radiant energy pulsating with a fierce intensity. The ghosts recoiled. They writhed in agony. Repelled by the brightness. They coalesced into a single, fiery entity - merging into a blazing inferno of otherworldly power.

Broken and battered, Lillie collapsed to her knees, the hard floor beneath her offering little comfort as she gasped for air, her throat raw from inhaling choking smoke.

Through tear-blurred vision, she could see the scorching monstrosity hovering, a menace above her. Its blistering form contorted and twisted in a grotesque dance of malevolence.

Lillie's chest tightened as she fought to stay conscious, her mind reeling from the intensity of the moment.

The room around her crackled with tension, thick with the stench of embers burning and the acrid tang of fright. Every fibre of her being screamed for release from the suffocating grip of the inferno, which threatened to consume her.

In spite of the overwhelming terror that she feared would overwhelm her, she clung to consciousness, striving for a way of escape.

Through the haze of smoke and fire, a beacon of light pierced the darkness. It illuminated the scene with its radiant glow. Within its brilliance, she again glimpsed the ethereal image of her sister. It appeared to pulse with a protective energy. Pushing back against the malevolent presence that sought to devour them both.

With trembling hands, she reached out towards her sister's spirit. Her fingers brushed its shimmering surface. In that moment, a surge of power shot through her, coursing through her veins like wildfire. It enveloped her in a safe shield, warding off the hostile entity, as it tried to destroy them.

Her body quivered with exhaustion and anguish. Drawing strength from her sibling's protection that surrounded her, her resolve was unwavered in the face of adversity. In that instant, she knew that no matter how dark the night may get, hope would always prevail.

The fiery being let out a deafening roar, its form writhing in agony as it struggled against the barrier of light. With a final, desperate effort, she focused all her energy on reinforcing the shield. Willing it to hold, stopping the relentless assault.

The entity grew weaker, its blazing shape flickering and fading until it was reduced to a wisp of smoke. With a last defeated hiss, it vanished into the ether, leaving behind only a persistent sensation of fear.

Exhausted and shaken, she dropped to the ground. Her body quivered from the exertion.

Before there was time to make sense of everything occurring in the bakery at Misthaven, time itself appeared to warp and distort. The walls began melting like wax under extreme heat. An erratic fluctuation of gravity played out in front of her. Her remaining surroundings collapsed into darkness.

With hesitation, she reached down and put her hands on the floor. It was cold, like concrete, and damp. A light drizzle begins to soak her clothes.

Looking up, she found herself in the town square, engulfed by fog. The overpowering smell of wet earth and salty sea water filled the air. Through the opaque mist, the twisted expressions on the faces of townspeople materialised. Their silent cries echoed in the uncomfortable quiet. Lillie's fingertips brushed the dampness of a lamppost as she hurried away from the bakery.

Navigating through the dense fog, the plaza transformed into a mosaic of unsettling sounds. Muffled footsteps danced around her; their origin hidden by the swirling mist. Shadows flitted in and out of view, elusive and ominous.

The overwhelming apprehension of the unknown weighed down every breath she took. The uncanny whispers, though faint, lingered, trailing after her like a haunting melody.

In the darkness, her senses were more acute. The rustle of fabrics and shuffle of feet startling her. Straining to see through the veil of fog, she stumbled, as it obscured her vision. It amplified her sense of vulnerability.

With each step forward, a disconcerting soundscape

engulfed her. A chorus of invisible dangers, accompanied it, lingering beyond reach. Moving with care; her nerves taut with apprehension. Unaware of what sinister presence could be lurking in the mist.

Stopping, she took a breath. Beside her two buildings overhung, the gap between them covered with a heavy overgrowth of ivy. Through the foliage, a faint welcoming glow radiated.

Drawn by the prospect of escaping her nightmares, she ventured into the narrow passage.

Strolling down the peculiar alleyway, she was peaceful. With a sense of relief, she cast her eyes around. The walls were engraved with ancient-looking symbols.

The pathway came to a dead end. With reluctance, she began to turn and go back.

A flash of blinding light immersed her. It faded, she shrieked at the sight. In front of her was the backyard of her childhood home. It was a place where she had spent countless hours playing and dreaming.

Except, something was different this time. The calmness she had been experiencing dissipated. An ominous tension built inside her. A sense of discomfort pressed down on her.

Looking out onto the once familiar garden, her eyes fell upon a group of shadowy figures. They gathered around under the orchard trees. Their faces were obscured by dark hoods. Weird chants drifted on the air, as they circled a makeshift shrine.

Watching in horror, she was unable to take her eyes off it. Someone raised a gleaming knife. Twisting it high above their head. Their voice soared in a fervent prayer to some unseen entity. The blade glinted in the dim light, casting long shadows across the ground.

With a sinking sensation in the pit of her stomach, she realised what was about to happen. This was no ordinary gathering - it was a ritual, a dark and twisted ceremony that threatened to unleash unspeakable horrors upon the world.

Try as she might, she could not turn away from the

gruesome scene unfolding, in spite of her disbelief that this was happening outside her innocent, childhood home.

Forcing a final break from the mesmerising vision, she ran. Her steps resounded, loud in the stillness of the night. As the hypnotic clutch slipped away from her, she picked up speed. A frantic endeavour to move away from the nightmare. The sound of the terrifying screams still boomed in her ears. Running through the streets she knew so well from her youth, she hastened.

It did not matter how fast she went; she could not shake the thought of dread that gripped her heart like a vice. The cult's presence loomed over her like a dark cloud.

Stumbling as she rounded a corner, she fell landing on her knees, her breath coming in ragged gasps. Tears streamed down her face as she struggled to understand f the horrors she had witnessed.

Now she was back in the Plaza. The fog still casting its grave spell.

In the obscured surroundings, a distant church bell tolled a mourning chime. The echoes chilled the air. The sombre tones resonated with her unease. Each ring amplified the ominous premonitions gripping her. The sense of impending dread intensified in the shadows.

In the heart of the mysterious fog, a dark figure materialised. Its presence more sensed than seen. It made a beckoning gesture that cut through the dense atmosphere.

Lillie, surrounded by the chilling mist, experienced an unearthly pull toward the fog-shrouded alleyways. Moving forward, the unseen hands of the fog touched her skin. It left a tingling sensation that bolted through the depths of her body. It seared and lingered with an electrifying intensity.

A flicker of movement caught her eye. It danced at the edge of her vision, taunting her with its elusiveness. A shiver went through her, an instinctive warning of impending danger.

Her unsteady hand extended towards the phenomenon against her will. Her pointed finger parted the fog, which began to lift as if being swallowed by an invisible vacuum cleaner. It was removing the whole scene.

In that eerie moment, a sense of weightlessness consumed her. Panic gripped her, as she saw reality slipping away. The ground dissolved into mist beneath her feet, pulling her into an unknown abyss. Overcome by anxiety, bewilderment flooded her thoughts.

The apparition vaporised in front of her, morphing with the fog. Lillie hung like a puppet, unable to take action. The plaza vanished before her eyes. With nothing solid to support her, she started to descend.

The landing was not what she expected, she glided to a gentle stop. Holding her breath, she opened her eyes. Blinking back sunshine, she peered out over the familiar sight of her garden.

A sigh left her. Jumping to her feet without hesitation, she headed for the door to her cottage, anxious to outrun the phantoms of her visions. Each step like navigating through a dreamscape, the rustle of leaves echoing the distant cries from her haunting experiences

Diving into her home, she slammed the door with such force that it made her jump. Staring back through the window, she threw the top bolt. Her face a picture of hysteria.

"Leave me alone, go away," she said, a wild expression in her eyes.

On her own in her sanctuary, she found no respite. Strange occurrences plagued her every moment. Objects moved of their own accord, shifting positions when she turned her back. Shadows elongated and twisted, taking on sinister shapes that spied on her. She could not shake the feeling of being trapped in a waking nightmare.

The following days unfolded in a surreal blend of reality and illusion, leaving her questioning the absolute essence of her existence.

Each corner of her cottage began to whisper secrets. The ceiling, covered in shimmering hues which formed cryptic symbols. The furniture trembled, and a voice, gentle yet insistent, drifted through the room, hinting at a connection beyond the material.

On one day, amidst the disconcerting interplay between the tangible and the supernatural, she escaped the house and sought solace within the confines of her garden.

Walking in the soft earth and listening to the rustling of leaves and the evening bird song, she found calmness.

Immersing herself in nature, Lillie's fingertips followed the subtle curves of every leaf, their edges shimmering in the sunlight. The plants, bathed in a floral glow, responding to her touch, their flowers swaying in a waltz.

In her mind this dance created an elusive link between her and the forces that held a relentless grip on her present situation. It intertwined the natural environment with the mysterious energies that encircled her.

A sudden fear gripped her. In her paranoia, she suspected the dancing of the shrubs may trigger another premonition. Sighing, she withdrew to the cottage, acknowledging that no safe place existed now.

That night, sleep swallowed her into a disorienting space where the boundary separating her world of premonitions and reality vanished.

Stood in the bedroom, a gust of wind blew through the room. Intensifying, it caused all the furniture to levitate. The mirror before her began to ripple like water, revealing Misthaven town centre. Trying to step back, she met a resistance that thrust her forward instead.

Flinching, she expected the slashing pane of glass. It did not come. To her surprise she stumbled into the labyrinthine alleys of Misthaven.

Her perceptions were engulfed by the fog's chilling touch. Shadowy figures whispered her name, the voices resonating now with familiarity.

Amid the gloomy landscape, an image materialised in her mind – an ancient well encircled by twisted trees, its surroundings echoing with murderous cries.

The sensation overwhelmed her. Her thoughts anxious, filled with despair. The fog thickened, wrapping her in oppressive darkness. It intensified the disconcerting atmosphere. The spectral figure, a ghostly silhouette, reappeared from her premonition, its form beckoning her closer.

Helpless to stop, she drifted towards it against her will. A menacing scene unfolded as she approached. The well of her earlier imaginings manifested itself in front of her.

A hooded figure emerged from the shadows, its voice a hushed hostile whisper. "Welcome to Misthaven," It murmured, sending shivers down her spine

The wind howled like a chorus of tormented souls. Dark, ominous clouds gathered overhead, blotting out the last remaining shreds of sunlight. Whispers of an impending doom echoed among the twisted branches of the hedgerow.

The well's overturned bucket spewed out a chilling stream of crimson blood. The pungent metallic scent assaulted her throat. The gruesome sight sent a cascade of terrifying tremors through her. It awakened her with a gasp.

The lingering sensations of dread and the horrific images remained with her. They merged the boundaries of the dream world and her waking reality.

Every day that went by added another level of complexity. Lillie spent most of it in her bedroom, terrified by the tsunami of premonitions and nightmares that flooded her life. As the days and nights went on, the line between them blurred. Being asleep and awake were blending into one.

One evening, as the fog outside reflected her internal anguish, Lillie sought refuge in music. Plugging in her earphones, she submerged herself in the soothing melodies of a piano concerto. Rachmaninoff's Prelude in C-sharp Minor played, but instead of calming her, the melody synchronised with the rapid dance of shadows on the floor.

Lost in the mystical sounds, Misthaven Island materialised before her. Shrouded in a sinister mist, it beckoned with a mysterious charm. The fog, like a phantom curtain, parted. The place emanated an indefinable energy that tugged at her core, promising elusive answers to the questions that haunted her.

As she submerged herself in the haunting tune, her senses tingled with a sensation that seemed to draw her closer to Misthaven Island. With a quiver in her fingers, she removed her earphones. The music dissolved into the air around her. In awe, she fixated on the spectral mirage of the island looming before her.

Even as the tentacles of anxiety crept up her spine and the uncertainty knotted in her stomach; a spark of resolve ignited within her mind. It was a determination that surged forth, fuelled by the need to confront the enigmatic mysteries veiled on Misthaven Island, to unravel the maze of dreams and visions that entrapped her life.

With a slow, steadying breath, she braced herself for what lay ahead. Her every movement spoke of her courage, a silent testament to the decision that would reshape the course of her life.

As the fog's weight slipped from her shoulders, she could not shake the residual doubts clawing at her mind, wondering. 'Can I really face what lies ahead?' The thought wavering her resolve even as she stepped forward.

The environment mirrored her inner turmoil, with the distant cries of seagulls echoing in the air.

The air was full off the briny scent of saltwater, undercut by the unmistakable tang of decay. It assaulted her senses and added to the atmosphere.

The island beckoned with its spectral allure, its shores shrouded in mist, its secrets lurking within the depths of its tangled forests.

The next morning, standing before the mirror, she studied her reflection. Memories of past struggles and lost loved ones flooded her mind. Each line etched on her face told a story. One of resilience in the face of adversity, a testament to the strength that had carried her through countless trials.

Yet, in her eyes, a spark of determination flickered, a silent vow to escape the visions that grasped her like the persistent fog.

Summoning the scant courage remaining, she reached for her phone. Dialling Aunt Helena's number, she thought about the burden of her decision. The sound of ringing began, set to speaker mode, the beeping echoed in her quiet cottage.

Aunt Helena answered. A strange buzzing came from the other end of the line. A voice spoke in a cryptic tone.

"You have shown spirit in choosing to go with your aunt. Be warned though - Misthaven Island holds secrets darker than you can imagine," it said. "Prepare yourself for a journey that will test your soul."

Her heart started to pound, and mind raced in confusion. Now thinking, she would be making a mistake going on this trip.

"Helena speaking," Aunt Helena said. Cutting into the alien announcement.

"Oh, high Aunt, err, it's Lillie," she said.

"Hello, darling. Lovely to hear from you," Aunt Helena said. "I do hope your calling to say you have decided to come away with me."

"Well, I've been giving it some thought, " Lillie said. "I have been stressed of late. It's affecting my mental health. It might be that a break is what I need."

"Just the tonic then, I'll get in touch with them," she said.

"Wait. Something strange happened before you picked up the phone. It was like a static voice. Did you hear it?" Lillie said. Regretting now that she had phoned.

"No, not a thing. Like you said, a bit of static," answered Helena.

"It's freaked me a little. Plus, other weird things have been happening during the last couple of weeks," said Lilli.

"All the more reason to have a little holiday. Don't you think?" said Aunt Helena. "I know it' is scary for you because you don't get out much, but just imagine the incredible adventures that await us. This is our chance for us to explore a place that has been untouched for decades."

Lillie listened; the concern evident in her voice. "What if something goes wrong? It is so remote; we could get stranded?"

Aunt Helena's tone softened, infused with reassurance.

"Nonsense My dear. Come on, I understand your worries, I will prepare for every possibility." She said. "Anyway, facing challenges is part of the thrill of adventure. We will navigate through them together. Like we always do."

Lillie hesitated, the uncertainty still lingering in her mind. "I don't know, aunty..."

Aunt Helena became more earnest, her words carrying conviction. "Trust me. I do think it will help you."

Lillie fell silent for a moment, contemplating her aunt's comments. At last, with a determined sigh, she spoke. "You're right. Let's do it. Let's go to Misthaven Island and make this journey our own."

Aunt Helena's joy was palpable through the phone. "That's my girl! I knew you would see it my way. Together, we will conquer any challenge that comes our way. Misthaven Island, here we come!"

With newfound determination, Lillie hung up the telephone, ready to embark on their trip.

CHAPTER FOUR

A week later, Aunt Helena arrived at Lillie's home.

The fire crackled in the hearth, casting dancing shadows across the room, Lillie sat huddled in her favourite armchair, a haunted expression etched on her face. Aunt Helena watched her niece with concern visible in her gentle eyes. "Dear, you appear troubled," she said her voice carrying a soothing tone.

Lillie let out a deep sigh. her gaze fixed upon the flickering flames. "It's these nightmares or whatever they are," she said, her confession tinged with frustration. "They're relentless, haunting me night after night."

Aunt Helena reached out and placed a comforting hand on hers "I'm sorry to hear that sweetheart," she said, with genuine sympathy. "Have you tried anything to alleviate them?"

Lillie nodded her head, her expression disturbed. "I've given everything a go. Meditation, warm milk before bed, even those herbal teas you suggested. Nothing seems to work."

Frowning, Aunt Helena's face appeared thoughtful. After a moment, she spoke again, her voice gentle yet determined. "Perhaps it's time sought a different approach. There are specialists. They could offer some insight. Have you spoken to your doctor?"

Lillie had the faintest hint of hope in her eyes. "No, I haven't. It sounds like a good idea though," she said, a sense of relief washing over her at the prospect of finding a solution. "Thank you. I don't know what I would do without you."

Aunt Helena beamed a warm smile, she gave Lillie's shoulder an affectionate squeeze.

"No need for thanks dear. We will get through this together," she said, her voice unwavering in its support. "Now, why don't we make some tea and try to relax? Dwelling on these nightmares won't help you."

Lillie smiled back at her aunt, gratitude filling her heart. "Yes, tea would be nice," she agreed, sensing hope ignite within her once more. With her aunty by her side, she knew she could face anything, even the darkest of dreams.

"You may feel better after our little break and when we get back, we will find you some help," Aunt Helena said

The next day, after another misty morning, Lillie and her aunt were setting off from the harbour. They were embarking on the first public crossing to Misthaven Island in over thirty years.

Still unsure it was the right thing to do, Lillie's stomach was churning. Staying at the cottage was, however, not an attractive option for her anymore. At home, the whispers descended on her with every mist that blew in. The premonitions and nightmares were increasing in quantity and bizarreness by the day. Whatever her visions had shown, she was certain she would discover the answer on the island.

The boat cruised across the serene expanse. The fog started to creep over the placid water's broad swath of vivid blue, changing it to a mysterious canvas of subdued greys and whites, with each wave being consumed by the mist.

With its bow making a ghostly trail amid the fog, it cut through the waves at a slow pace, causing it to part in soft murmurs. Lillie was disheartened that the fog was back.

Eyes full of terror, she gave her aunt a quick glance. Aunt Helena did not seem to notice. Turning away. Lillie stared into the murky water, scared that the voices in the fog would reappear. Slowing her breathing, she focussed on the gentle lapping of the sea on the hull and the sporadic creak of the stern.

The horizon had disappeared, replaced by a smooth transition between the fog and the ocean, leaving them alone in a quiet, dreamlike environment.

It took patience and attention for the skipper to navigate this weird realm. The boat was now inching closer to its destination, a lone craft crossing the channel. Lillie had spent the whole time jumping at every sound. Imagining it was the whispers again, pleading out of the fog.

As the ferry sliced through the dissipating fog, the veil that had cloaked their surroundings lifted, revealing a rugged shoreline that jutted, in defiance, from the mist like a spectral apparition. The silhouette of their intended location materialised against the backdrop of the vanishing haze.

With an intense gaze, she watched as the island emerged from the mist, its contours unchanged by the passage of time since her last encounter with it.

With one breath, she filled her lungs with the salty tang of the sea-infused air. As sunlight pierced through the lingering mist, its gentle rays softened the jagged edges of the towering cliffs that bordered the shoreline.

With each wisp of vapor that disappeared, her apprehension melted away, replaced by a sense of tranquillity that settled far within her soul. A smile played upon her lips as she basked in the warmth of the sun filtering through the canopy of trees that crowned the cliff's edge, casting dappled shadows on the beach below.

Following in the shadow of her aunt, Lillie ascended the weathered steps of the short jetty. The timbers made a soft groan beneath their weight. Above, a chorus of seabirds soared in lazy circles. Their distant cries continued on the gentle breeze that whispered secrets of the sea.

Their host, Miles Beaumont, was waiting for them. Thinking of the newspaper article she had seen him pictured in, she recognised him.

"Welcome. My first guests, how exciting. Come, come along," he said, waving his hands around in frantic gestures, pushing his portly belly out until it nearly popped a button on his poor fitting, pinstripe suit.

"Miles Beaumont I presume?" Aunt Helena said.

Lillie slunk behind her, her head lowered, not making eye contact

"You can only be Helena and Lillie. You are the first mainlanders to step on my island for thirty years?" he said, opening his arms in a welcoming gesture.

"Privileged, I'm sure." Aunt Helena said, with delight in her voice.

"Your chariot awaits madam," he said. Laughing as he held his hand out towards a golf buggy. "The poshest transport we have, well the only type unless you can ride a horse."

They climbed aboard. Miles talked with enthusiasm all the way up the narrow-rugged track. He revealed a wealth of knowledge about the island and its history.

"Helena, have you ever heard about the ancient ruins scattered across the island?" Miles asked, his eyes alight with excitement.

Helena, intrigued, answered. "No, tell us more about them."

"Well, legend has it that they date back centuries, possibly even to the time of the early European settlers." Miles said, gesturing towards the rough landscape around them. "They're believed to have been part of a thriving civilization that vanished in mysterious circumstances."

Lillie, now full of engagement for the conversation, said. "That's fascinating! What happened to them?"

Miles shrugged. "No one knows for sure. Some say it was a natural disaster, while others believe it was due to conflicts with mainland tribes. Regardless, the ruins serve as a reminder of the island's rich and complex history."

Helena's eyes widened with interest. "And what about more recent events? Anything significant?"

Miles nodded. Oh yes, during World War II, this island played a crucial role as a training camp for Morse code operators and a secret base for codebreakers. It was a hub of clandestine activity, with operatives deciphering enemy communications to gain valuable intelligence."

Lillie gasped, "That's incredible! I had no idea this island held such secrets."

"There's more," Miles said with eagerness. "In the Elizabethan era, this island housed a watchtower that participated in a pivotal part in history. It was here that the Spanish Armada was first spotted, and a swift message was sent to Sir Francis Drake in Plymouth, alerting him to the impending invasion."

As they continued their journey up the narrow track, Helena paid close attention, captivated by Miles' tales of the island's past and its historical significance.

Lillie's mind drifted off. A sudden whistle of wind made a branch creak above their heads. Pulled from her daydream Lillie was startled and peered up.

"Yes, we get some raging winds out here some winters but that's a tame gust just those old trees groaning making it sound worse than it actually is," he said, laughing, sounding pleased with himself.

They were nearing the manor now. It was smaller than Lillie remembered, charming yet unassuming. Its whitewashed walls, weathered by the inclement weather that swept up the channel. Light reflected off symmetric bay windows which were divided by a central entrance and a sun-bleached porch.

Miles Beaumont helped them with their luggage as he led the way to their rooms, they were adjacent, in the attic. Lillie gazed out of the window and sighed, there were views all the way down the tree lined driveway and out across the water towards the south Devon coastline.

CHAPTER FIVE

As they settled in, a sudden power outage plunged the manor into darkness. The howling wind outside intensified, causing the trees to thrash against the windows. Lillie and Helena exchanged uneasy glances, as a sinister sense of foreboding crept over them.

They went to the landing. Miles was approaching the stairs from the opposite direction. There was an abrupt change in his mood, as he saw them. He fumbled with a flashlight. His eyes moved, in a nervous motion, around the house.

In the glow of the torch, he guided them downstairs to the sitting room. A fire crackled in the hearth, causing shadows on the walls to dance. The atmosphere became tense with anticipation.

"Sit a moment," he said. "I will have to switch the batteries over. Please don't worry. We generate lots of power through the solar panels, there are always back-ups with full charge."

Helena gave him a relieved glance. In contrast, Lillie's complexion had become pale, the situation unnerving her.

Waving his arms in an animated gesture Miles disappeared to rectify the energy supply. A few minutes went by and the lights in the lounge buzzed on. Lillie exhaled a breath of calm.

An hour later, they took their places for dinner. The warm glow of candlelight casting a soft ambiance over the room. The table was set with fine china and polished silverware. The centrepiece a bouquet of fresh flowers from the garden.

They began their meal, the conversation flowing with ease. The earlier tension subsided in the comfort of pleasant company and delicious food.

Miles regaled them with stories of the island's history. His passion evident in every word. The aroma of roast lamb filled the air, accompanied by the delicate flavours of seasonal vegetables and herbs.

The atmosphere over dinner was one of warmth and camaraderie. And as they savoured each bite, Lillie felt a sense of gratitude for the hospitality of their host.

Miles leaned forward; his voice bearing the impact of previous generations. "My family's ties to this island run deep. My ancestors were not only residents here; they were guardians of secrets, keepers of knowledge that helped turn the course of war."

He paused, allowing the gravity of his words to sink in before continuing. "During World War II, they served with the codebreakers, learning to decipher enemy communications. They worked with unwavering dedication. It was a perilous time, but also one of extreme courage and sacrifice."

Lillie's eyes widened with interest as she listened. Her curiosity piqued by Miles' revelation. Hearing his passion for the subject, she could sense remnants of a bygone era that still lingered in the air.

"My ancestors," he said, his voice steady. "Made a solemn vow to protect the secrets they uncovered, to ensure that the sacrifices given during those tumultuous years would never be forgotten. I would like to preserve the island's historical story now. I have the same feeling of responsibility and loyalty."

"That is why I sacrificed the house on the mainland, when I was hit with an inheritance tax bill," he said. "By visiting you also are doing your bit to conserve this place. For that I am grateful."

He raised his glass. "A toast, to Misthaven, guardian of the Devon coast."

As he spoke, Lillie felt a new respect for their host, a deeper understanding of the significance of their visit. Their glasses clinked over the dining table.

As Miles's remarks trailed off into the night, Lillie's belief in her decision to come to the island was renewed.

The next morning dawned bright and clear. For the first time in weeks, she awoke well rested, after a night free from nightmares or visions.

At breakfast, Miles offered to take Lillie and Helena on a tour around the island to explore its hidden nooks and crannies further.

They set off up rugged paths. They wound their way through lush greenery and ancient woodlands. The island lay bathed in golden sunlight.

Their first stop was the ruins of the island's crumbling quay. Its weathered stones bore witness to centuries of maritime activity. Lillie ran her fingers along the rough surface, imagining the bustling harbour that once thrived there.

"It fell into disrepair in the fifties. After the MOD left," Miles said. "My family could never afford the repairs. It was cheaper to build the new jetty on the south of the island. The one you arrived at."

"Well, perhaps if you make a success of opening the island up, it could be a future project for you," Aunt Helena said.

"I would like to show you where the codebreakers were based. If you are interested. It's a bit of a time warp," Miles said.

"That would be fascinating," Aunt Helena answered. " Is it far?"

"No. About a fifteen-minute walk up that path," he said, pointing to the rough begging's of a cut out track. "It's quite steep and a little overgrown in places, but it's manageable. It's worth the climb just for the view. After, we can make our way down the other side of the hill, in the direction of the house."

They ventured up the trough track. pushing back overgrowth and branches when it blocked their way. As the trees cleared at the summit Miles showed them a long-forgotten operations room, filled with dusty equipment.

A flash of movement caught her eye. Blinking in surprise, a picture unfolded before her. In the poor light of the room, she saw the uniformed figures of radio operators huddled over their devices. Their fingers flew across the keys as they deciphered messages.

The scene faded as quick as it had appeared. Leaving Lillie shaken but intrigued by the glimpse into the island's past. Moving, she turned to Miles. Her eyes grew with wonder. "Did you see that?" she whispered, her voice barely above a breath.

"The echoes of history are strong on this island," he said. His gaze distant. "It is said that the spirits of those who once walked these paths still linger, bound by duty and devotion to their cause."

In that moment, standing amidst the relics of times gone by, Lillie felt a renewed appreciation for the island and its rich heritage.

Glancing over the dusty equipment; her interest heightened. Miles stood beside her, his expression a mixture of reverence and nostalgia.

"Wow," Lillie said, running her fingers over the old apparatus. "This is incredible."

Miles nodded, a faint smile tugging at the corners of his lips. "It's like stepping back in time, isn't it? This room holds so many stories."

Helena, too, seemed captivated by the scene before them. "To think that this room played such a crucial role during the war. It's truly remarkable."

Miles' stare lingered on the vintage radio set; his voice tinged with emotion. "My ancestors spent countless hours in this room, decoding messages, intercepting enemy transmissions. They were unsung heroes, an endless effort to ensure the safety of our country."

Lillie glanced up at him, struck by the depth of his words. "It must be an incredible legacy preserve."

"It is," Miles said. "But it's also a responsibility, to honour their memory, to pass on the stories of those who came before us."

Lillie entered a poorly light office located at the rear of the structure. The smell of mildew and old books hung in the air. A strange sensation passed through her.

It was as if the room itself held memories. Secrets whispered among the shadows. Trying to dispel the feeling, she shook her head, but it clung to her like a stubborn cobweb, tangling her thoughts in its intricate strands.

In the midst of her exploration, Lillie's gaze drifted toward a corner of the room. There stood an antique armchair, its once-grand upholstery now faded and worn. Then something happened - a vision, swift and jarring. In the chair sat a man. His form slumped back. A solitary bullet lodged in his chest. His eyes were closed, as if in peaceful repose. Yet, the pallor of death clung to his features.

With a gulp, Lillie felt her heart racing. Blinking, she tried to shake off the vision. However, it lingered in her thoughts like a haunting spectre. The room seemed to close in around her. The picture of the unseen tragedy playing out in her mind.

Shaken, Lillie backed out of the room, with haste. Her fingers trembled as she fumbled with the door handle. Not able to explain the vision, she did not want to dwell on its implications.

With a final, uneasy glance across the room, she hurried out. The echo of her footsteps following her. The scene of the slumped figure haunted her every step. A chilling reminder that even here, she was not safe from visions.

"Are you alright Lillie," Miles said from behind her.

Turning to face him, she said. "Yes, I got a little spooked. It must have been a dangerous time."

Unable to rid herself of the last trace of the vision, Lillie became quiet as they continued their tour.

Returning to the south side of the island, they came upon hidden coves and secluded beaches, each one beautiful. On the clifftops there was a network of ancient mounds and stone circles.

On their way back to the manor house, they came across a medieval well, tucked away in a grove of trees. Lillie was not able to identify it, although she sensed it seemed familiar.

Another flash of a vision startled Lillie. This time, she saw a hooded figure standing by the well, their face obscured in shadow as they gazed down at the woodland floor.

The vision faded quickly, leaving Lillie breathless and uncertain of what she had seen. Moving, she faced Miles, her heart pounding in her chest. "Did you see that? There was someone by the well," she asked, her voice trembling with uncertainty.

Miles' expression was grave as he shook his head, his eyes dull with concern. "There are many mysteries on this island," he said. "And some secrets are best left undisturbed."

CHAPTER SIX

After joining Miles and her aunt for dinner, Lillie made her excuses. Seeing them deep in conversation, she retired to her room for an early night.

As dusk fell over the island, casting long shadowy areas on the landscape, Lillie found herself unable to sleep. Restless and unsettled, she tossed and turned in her bed, her mind plagued by visions of dark figures lurking in the shadows.

Despite Misthaven Island being peaceful, and the evening pleasant, a sense of unease gnawed at Lillie's thoughts. Each creak of the old manor house echoed with a haunting resonance, amplifying her anxiety.

Attempting to throw off the oppressive weight pressing down on her chest, she thought of the beauty of her surroundings and the comfort of her aunt's presence in the adjacent room. But the spectre of terror refused to be banished, its tendrils wrapping around her mind with an iron grip.

With a heavy sigh, Lillie accepted that she would not be getting much sleep tonight. Rising from her bed and making her way to the window, she drew back the curtains to reveal the moonlit landscape bathed in silver light.

Outside, the shadows danced in the gentle breeze, their forms shifting and twisting in the darkness. Watching in silence; her heart sank, weighty with a sense of unease that was difficult to fully overcome.

As she gazed out into the night, a flicker of determination sparked within her. With renewed resolve, she whispered a silent prayer for strength and courage, knowing that whatever trials lay ahead, she would face them head-on. Returning to her bed, and content, sleep came with ease.

The sound of arguing woke her. Confused, she found herself under the trees, on the edge of the driveway.

Looking through branches to a clearing she could see an old well - she recognised it from there tour. There was something else familiar about it to her, but she could not recollect.

Her brow furrowed in confusion, unsure of how she had got there. A subtle revelation crept across her face, her eyes widening as understanding unfurled in the depths behind her glazed eyes - a premonition.

Trying to move a branch to get a better view, her hand betrayed her.

A sudden quiver coursed through her fingers like leaves in a gentle breeze. Her shoulders now bore the tremors of its own invisible storm. Her eyes flickered with uncertainty. Her fright was causing her knees to tremble and almost give way. Each tremor that ripped through her painted a picture of the turmoil raging in her mind.

The rain was heavy, she tried to peer through it but saw no one. The arguing sounded closer. The high wind made it impossible to hear what was being shouted.

The deep vegetation stole the light from the trees, casting swirling shadows in front of her even in the daylight, making visibility difficult.

Attempting to move, she found herself motionless, like a bystander. In the dense silence of the forest, a muted gasp escaped Lillie's lips, a soundless echo of horror.

The silhouette of two figures ran into the clearing. One of them stopped in an abrupt stumble, a graceless falter, and then a swift descent as the second figure, a distinct masculine shape, lunged, forcing the other to the ground.

Another scream clawed at her throat, a visceral urge

to release the unspoken terror. Closing her eyes against the unfolding nightmare, she tried to exit the premonition.

A sudden burst of light fractured the obscurity, not sunlight but a strong beam akin to a stage spotlight, illuminating the grim spectacle. In the fleeting brilliance of lightning, her horrified gaze locked onto the lifeless form of Miles Beaumont, sprawled on the floor of the clearing.

His assailant, face veiled by a shadowy hood, cast a menacing shadow over him, a chilling silhouette.

Placing her hand on her cheek, she blinked, in an effort to remove the premonition. When she opened her eyes, she witnessed Miles Beaumont's body being dragged to the well.

"Lillie, Lillie!" said Aunt Helena.

Lillie sat up in bed. Turning, she saw her aunt was next to her holding her hand.

"Lillie, you had a bad dream. You were screaming," Aunt Helena said.

"No, it was more than that," Lillie said, her voice trembled as she spoke. "Miles is going to be murdered."

"Nonsense, you've just had a nightmare." Aunt Helena said, her composure calm as she reached out her other hand to her.

"No, no. I need to warn Miles," Lillie said, pushing past her aunt and bolting out of the door.

"Lillie. Where are you going?"

"Miles, Miles," she screamed.

Lillie's footsteps reverberated through the house, a rapid drumming on the weathered pine floorboards as she bounded across the landing.

The door to Miles' bedroom loomed ahead, yawning open as if inviting her to give up its secrets.

"Come on, Lillie stop worrying. Miles is fine," Aunt Helena said, from the far end of the shadow filled attic.

"No, no, it's happening again. I'm to late," she said, beginning to cry, as she looked around the empty room.

"What do you mean?" Aunt Helena said.

Pushing past Aunt Helena, she ran for the stairs. "I have to find him and warn him."

"Lillie please, Miles is here ..." Aunt Helena shouted after her.

The words from her aunt faded into a distant murmur as Lillie sprinted through the shadows of the downstairs hallway.

The dimness surrounded her like a shroud. Swift and determined, she reached the front door in a heartbeat.

Beyond the threshold, a silent drama unfolded. The fog, a spectral presence, slithered up the driveway. An ethereal blanket obscuring an ominous scene. It danced through the trees, weaving its threads to conceal the boundary, where they gave way to the clearing which housed the well.

Now, caught between urgency and trepidation, she sensed the influence of numerous unseen perils, concealed beneath the mist.

The bitter chilly rain slashed at Lillie's face. Wiping it from her face. she sprinted down the drive. Tiny stones of the unsurfaced track cut into her feet like biting ants, before she leaped over to the grass verge and vanished into the misty wooded area.

"The Well," came the whispers, united now instead of a cacophonous babble

At the clearing's boundary, Lillie crumpled to the ground. The damp from the earth seeping through the fabric of her nightdress.

A vice gripped her chest, each breath a desperate gasp for icy threads of relief. The atmosphere became dense with a cold that clawed at her lungs, she fought to draw in air.

Her heart, an erratic percussion, echoed in her ears. For a moment it eclipsed the sound of the wind and rain that was coursing through the trees. Every beat reverberated, a resounding drum.

To clear her view, she pulled a branch to one side. All she could see were shadows dancing across the undergrowth.

"The Well, the well," came the whispers, louder now.

Crawling to the base of an ancient oak tree, she sat against the trunk. Its abrasive bark cut into her back. Shivering, she drew her knees up to her chest.

A flood of tears, mixed with the rainwater descended her cheeks, rushing and plummeting like a waterfall. As she held her head in her hand, the sobbing flowed in an unstoppable and overwhelming display of relief, after seeing the clearing was empty.

The rain stopped, she attempted to remove the moisture from her face with her wet sleeve, but it provided no respite.

"The well, the well," The voices said, insistent. Lillie tried to block them out.

Starting to collect her thoughts, her breathing returned to a regular pace.

Rising from the base of the oak tree, she was cold and confused, beginning to doubt that it was a premonition at all. It was a nightmare like Aunt Helena had said, but Miles had not been at the house, which was odd.

"Where could he be?" she mumbled the question aloud. "Why would he be out of the house so early on a stormy morning like this."

"The well, the well, go to the well," now a solo whispering voice in the fog.

Aunt Helena would know what to do, she reasoned, but the most important thing is that he is all right.

She was about to retreat a step towards the house when a deafening clap of thunder rumbled through the air. The sound waves vibrated through her body. She froze, staring down at the well while lightning flashed above. The light filtered through the top of the canopy like search lights hitting the ground.

Lillie put her hand to her mouth – the wooden structure that had once covered the well was propped up against its granite side.

"Yes, the well. see the well," the whisper somehow blocked out the noise of the storm, becoming clear and coherent.

"Yeah, okay," she shouted. "I know."

Lillie's entire frame trembled with an involuntary shudder. She crossed the clearing with caution. Upon reaching the well, her fingers met the cool, unyielding surface of the hard stone creation.

Taking a rapid breath, she summoned the courage to peer into the dark chasm below. The darkness stared back, an impenetrable void, which swallowed the air she was breathing.

The fog dissipated before her, unveiling a macabre revelation. As the thunder roared, and lightning illuminated the scene, intensifying the downpour into a torrential deluge, she discerned the silhouette of a lifeless body, draped face down in the well.

Stepping back, she recoiled, letting out a sharp gasp, unleashing an otherworldly scream that reverberated through the trees. Despair painted her expression as she scrutinised the depths, half-expecting the shadows to mock her senses.

Breaking free from her petrified state, she turned away. Stumbling away from the well, she disappeared into the embrace of the surrounding woodland. Branches lashed against her face. She became disoriented as she sought escape. Panic surged, blurring her sense of direction.

The manor house eluded her sight. A torrent of thoughts inundated her mind. In a frenzied dash, she sprinted up the driveway. Uncertainty and desperation propelled her forward.

She rounded a corner in her frantic race. There was the house, the door still open. Diving onto the porch, she collided with someone coming the other way.

She staggered startled by what she could see. It was a shock to many; her head went light; her legs gave out and she fell to the ground in front of Miles Beaumont.

CHAPTER SEVEN

The disorienting fog of unconsciousness lifted. Still lost in a cloud of confusion, Lillie stared at the ceiling. Her temples pulsed with a persistent ache as she blinked away the lingering daze.

She tried to piece together her surroundings. Above her worried faces loomed, concern that flickered in and out of focus.

Miles Beaumont crouched next to her, expressing genuine worry, The lines on his face showing the anxiety, which mirrored Lillie's own. The vision was clearing from her mind.

"What happened?" he said, his eyes dilating. "Where have you been?"

Getting up, her thoughts were consumed by the vivid visions of the body in the well. Lightheaded she lay back down.

Staring at Miles, her eyes saucers of fear, she said. "The well... someone's in the well! I thought it was you. I saw you."

Miles exchanged a bewildered glance with Aunt Helena, who was sat on the porch floor beside her.

"What are you talking about, sweetie?" Aunt Helena said.

A raspy hitch caught in Lillie's throat. "Someone in the well, at the clearing, they're... they're dead."

Aunt Helena's expression softened. She placed a kind hand on her shoulder. "It's okay, dear. There's no one in the well, it was just a dream."

She frowned at Aunt Helena. " I did see it! it was so vivid..."

Her heart galloped racing with disbelief; a wild drumbeat pounded in her torso. Her brow furrowed, and she fixed her stare on Aunt Helena. "I did see it! It was real." she said, the words hanging in Aunt Helena's mind.

Miles helped her to her feet. His eyes filled with concern. "Let's go back inside, out of this storm. You're cold and shaking."

Lillie allowed them to guide her back into the warmth of the house. Her thoughts, however, remained fixated on the haunting images she had witnessed moments before. She knew what she had seen, in the well and in the premonition.

Nestled into a chair by the fireplace, she pulled a blanket around her trembling frame.

The rain continued to drum as it hit the windows. The wind outside howled, nature's fury playing against the tense backdrop within.

Aunt Helena moved with purpose, creating a ritual of comfort. Hot tea simmered, its aroma mingling with the lingering tension. She circled, a soothing presence in the room, intent on both warming Lillie's chilled body and easing the frayed edges of her nerves.

Casting an uneasy glance toward Miles, Lillie said. "Miles, why were you out so early?"

He hesitated, glancing with caution towards Aunt Helena.

"Lillie," Aunt Helena cut in. "Miles hasn't left the house all night."

"How can, you be sure?" Lillie objected.

"I assure you, I haven't Lillie," he said. Not making eye contact with her as he spoke. "I will walk up to the well when it is light. I can tell you though there cannot be a body in the well, there is no one else on this island apart from us and our other guests who are safe, all tucked up in bed."

Lillie nodded with a determination that mirrored the relentless pace of her thinking. Her mind, bustling, unable to slow.

There lingered within her a constant belief that the situation held depths not revealed in full. The urgency of her premonition persisted, a haunting that she refused to be demoted to the realm of a mere dream.

The storm outside continued releasing its wrath. An unspoken tension clung to the atmosphere within the house. There was an overpowering sense of apprehension and unresolved questions in the air. Lillie's thoughts, like persistent currents, kept returning to the well—the eerie vision left an unforgettable mark on her.

With concern on her face, Aunt Helena came over to her. "Lillie, you need to rest. It's been a trying night."

Sleep remained a distant notion for Lillie, banished by the relentless pursuit of answers. The images refused to be subdued—they demanded validation or dismissal.

Sipping her tea, the comforting warmth spreading through her, she attempted to drown the lingering unease. A strange residue caught her attention at the cup's base, it teased her curiosity. Before she could voice her query, an unexpected drowsiness descended like a leaden curtain.

Her eyelids, weighted with exhaustion, succumbed to gravity, and her head dipped forward in surrender to the encroaching sleep.

Aunt Helena wasted no time in guiding Lillie up to her room, offering a supporting arm around her shoulder.

"You need some rest, dear. Let's get you to bed," she said.

Lillie's protests were feeble, her mind foggy. The effects of whatever had tainted her tea dulled her senses. It left her in a state of muted resistance.

She caught Aunt Helena's reassuring smile, in her final moments of awareness. Consciousness went and darkness descended. She succumbed to the embers of the dying fire in her thoughts.

Lillie stood once more at the clearing's edge, the ominous well looming before her like a silent sentinel. This time, the abyss below held no lifeless form, only the tumultuous sounds of the stormy night echoing in the air.

Exhaustion weighed on her, confusion apparent as she questioned the essence of her reality. Was this another dream, a vision, or an hallucination induced by whatever sedative that had been in her tea?

With a hesitant turn, she found herself confronted by the unexpected presence of Miles Beaumont. An involuntary shiver ran through her. His unreadable expression added an unnerving layer to the mysterious scene that was playing out in the clearing.

"Miles.... what's happening?" she said.

"Run, run, Lillie, run," came the whispers.

He remained silent, staring at her. She tried to move away, but panic held her there. It surged within her as she realised, she could not escape.

He maintained an unsettling silence, a hypnotic glare. It became futile, as if time had solidified to keep her captive.

The world, once coherent, warped into a disjointed tapestry of shadows and echoes. A pervasive dread descended upon her, an oppressive cloak tightening its grip with each passing moment.

Miles watched, his eyes keeping hers fixed in a mesmerising, transparent beam.

A sudden, forceful awakening propelled Lillie into reality. Her heart hammering, a wild animal attempting to break free from its cage of ribs that entrapped it. Darkness dominated the room, with regular interruptions by the haunting flashes of lightning that painted erratic patterns on the windows.

Driven by urgency, she sprinted to the door, a frantic effort to get out. Yet, her efforts were thwarted; the door, an immovable barrier, a menacing lock stopped her from getting out.

Panic surged through her as she rattled the handle, her voice echoing through the empty hallway. "Aunt Helena! Miles!" There was no response.

Peering through the window, Lillie strained to catch a sign of anyone amidst the raging storm. The howling wind proved an unrelenting battlefield, drowning out any potential cries for help. A gnawing terror tightened its grip as the realisation dawned— she was alone, imprisoned within the walls of her room.

Lillie's thoughts raced, attempting to unravel the enigma unfolding around her. Was it a mere extension of her dream, or did something more ominous lurk in the dimness? The unsettling horror from her nightmare persisted, driving her to seek a way out and to discover the truth.

Her hands trembled in a frantic attempt to search the room, desperate for any sign of an exit. Turning back to the door, a chilling understanding struck - the lock remained steadfast, and her sole companions were the unrelenting storm and the oppressive silence within the house.

Tears streamed down her face. Helplessness consumed her. Collapsing onto the bed, she succumbed to a torrent of emotions, believing she was abandoned. In the end, fatigue became a heavy weight on her, and she drifted to sleep, the storm's tumultuous symphony accompanying her into the realm of dreams.

CHAPTER EIGHT

With abrupt force, Lillie awoke. Startled, her heart raced. Confused at what had woken her, she peered around the room. Despite the bad weather's relentless presence, the room seemed peaceful, now lit by the gentle morning light streaming through the window. Hastening to the door, she turned the handle, with a shaking hand. To her surprise, the door swung open easily.

Lines of confusion furrowed her face as she entered the corridor. She descended the stairs with caution. The incidents of the previous night continued to whisk in her mind. Upon entering the dining area, the awkwardness of the atmosphere was evident.

Lillie took her seat at the table, making furtive glances at Aunt Helena, who gave her a small, knowing nod. There was a tangible tension in the air, an unspoken understanding that something was amiss.

Aunt Helena bustled around, setting the breakfast cutlery while Miles sat at far end of the room, he appeared engrossed in some paperwork. He tensed as Lillie walked in, followed by the occasional expressionless glance.

Miles claimed to have gone to the well earlier that day. He reported no signs of a body. The way Aunt Helena carried herself suggested that she had some misgivings. The time then passed in strained silence.

When they were alone for a moment, Aunt Helena drew

Lillie aside, her voice quiet and urgent. " I was with Miles last night until you woke up after your bad dream. We sat up talking right into the early hours, but something is not adding up about him. He does not remember certain conversations we had online before coming here. It is as if..."

Her words trailed off, the seriousness of the scenario overwhelming them both. Lillie's mind was filled with distrust. Her thoughts 'Is Miles concealing something? Could he have planned this entire thing?'

Aunt Helena's expression hardened with determination. "I need to check the well myself. Something tells me there's more to this than meets the eye."

Aunt Helena headed out; Lillie's anxiety intensified. She could not get over the haunting atmosphere of the dream. The ominous presence of Miles in it confused her.

Coming to the island had not stopped the visions tormenting her. Confusion filled her mind. If it was a premonition and there was no body in the well, then Miles was still in danger. If there was a body in the well, then as usual she was to late to change what she had prophesied, but who was dead at the bottom of the well. 'What was the point of having a gift of seeing the future if you could never act on it.' she thought as she paced the room.

She was torn between confronting Miles and waiting for Aunt Helena's return.

When Aunt Helena came back, her face was grave, her features etched with concern.

"There's a body in the well, Lillie. You were right. How did you know?" she asked.

Lillie's blood ran cold at the confirmation of her worst fears.

"The dream," she replied, sarcasm in her voice, knowing no one had listened to her.

Aunt Helena had not waited for an answer, she wasted no time; she turned her attention to Miles, noticing his appearance had shifted, he was now uneasy, his gaze flickering around the room.

With a resolute tone, Aunt Helena addressed Miles,."Miles, we need to talk about the inconsistencies in your story regarding the well. You said you checked it and found nothing, but we know otherwise."

Miles remained composed, he said. "I understand your concern, but I didn't want to alarm anyone if it was not necessary. I did contact the authorities when I realised something was amiss. However, due to the dense fog, they couldn't confirm when it would be safe to make the crossing to the island. I was advised to ensure no one leaves until they arrive."

Aunt Helena and Lillie exchanged puzzled looks. Their expressions were coloured with a mixture of relief and confusion. The realisation that Miles had acted, tempered the agitation in the room, yet questions still lingered about the unfolding situation.

The atmosphere remained charged with uncertainty. Despite Miles's explanation, doubts persisted, and the fog surrounding the secluded island now appearing as a veil of unease.

They made their way to the lounge. Both were quiet in reflection, as they grappled with the revelation. The sense of confinement on the isolated island grew more profound. The unresolved circumstances a heavy burden baring down on them.

Lillie was conflicted between gratitude for Miles' cautious actions and a lingering suspicion that he was not being truthful. The serene haven they had sought, had transformed into a place fraught with unanswered questions. It left them in the unsettling grip of a mystery.

"Do you believe him Aunt," she said. Making a deliberate turn in her direction so as not to alert Miles to her suspicions.

"Not a word of it, but why would he lie about something like this?" she answered, her posture sharp and confident, but her eyes betrayed her panic.

The sense of approaching danger thickened. The harsh reality of these circumstances crashed over Lillie.

"I have spoken with him many times since I made the booking," Aunt Helena said. "However, last night, on occasion, when I mentioned some of the topics we had discussed in our chats, he would change the subject, or the answer did not fit. He did not appear to be as self-assured in person. Now it seems even more odd."

"What if he hasn't phoned the police?" Lillie said, a solitary tear running down her face.

"We cannot be sure. So, we must check," she said, a glint of hope now in her eyes.

"The only phone in the house is in here," she pointed an oak bureau, which was in the centre of the far wall. "Go find Miles and watch him closely, don't let him in here."

With that she strode, determinedly across the thick, regal carpet. Passing Lillie, she shooed her away with a hand gesture.

Aunt Helena reached the antique piece of furniture, her hand shook as she picked up the receiver. With a steadying breath, she dialled the emergency number. She had the impression that time was moving slowly. Every digit resounded in the silent room; her whole body was now shaking in the fraught tension.

She could hear it ringing at the other end. Her heart raced, a hummingbird trying to escape from her chest. Without warning, footsteps sounded behind her, and she whirled around to see Miles standing at the entrance to the room, his expression unreadable. Taken by surprise, her throat gave way to a gasp.

Miles spoke in a calm tone, though there was a trace of suspicion in his voice. "What are you doing, Helena?" he said.

"Emergency, what service do you require?" The operator asked.

Regaining her composure in a beat, she forced a composed smile.

"Just making a call, dear. Everything's fine," she said.

Still, Miles's manner was reserved as he moved in closer.

"Hello, emergency, what service do you require?" The operator repeated.

Aunt Helena moved her head a little, so that Miles was unable to see the receiver. She gave the phone a gentle tap.

"Can you speak? Are you in danger?" Unperturbed by the

silent call, the operator continued.

Miles came closer.

"May I ask who?" he said.

"You are through to the police." Came an automated voice.

Aunt Helena shuddered with anxiety, on hearing the recorded message. She breathed, long and hard, trying to calm herself.

Quietly, with the slightest tremble in her speech, she said. "I am just trying to get through to the water taxi to book our transport back to the mainland. Like you said I could. Remember?"

"Press five on your keypad, if you need police call management." The automated recording went on to say.

Aunt Helena reacted immediately by pressing the number five key.

"Of course, but you don't have to leave today, right?" Miles said, remaining calm, but his eyes were squinting, a scowl across his face. His usual indecipherable body language penetrated.

"You are through to police control, what is the nature of the emergency?"

She was relieved to hear a real person again on the other end of the phone. She stared straight at Miles and sighed.

"It is this thing about the dead man in the well. It' shook Lillie up. I am scared for her mental health," she said.

Miles' face relaxed. He moved his head slightly.

"But not today, right?" he said.

The operator offered another closed question. "Is there someone in the room with you, do you feel threatened by them?"

Still looking directly at Miles, Aunt Helena said. "Yes, now."

Miles held his hands out, his previous suspicions gone, "Come on Helena, we are just getting to know each other. Last night was lovely, I am sure you agree. Well until your niece had a funny turn."

"Can you confirm you are on Misthaven Island?" The call handler said.

"Yes," Aunt Helena said, addressing Miles but hoping the operator would here it as her answer.

"Please consider staying a bit longer," Miles said, as he shifted on his feet in frustration.

"Are you able to get away from the person that is with you or off the island?" The operator asked, not faltering in her confidence.

"No, I can't, I can't get off this island," Aunt Helena replied.

Her sudden spluttered outburst, like machine gun fire, confirmed Miles' suspicions, His face flushed with anger.

Aunt Helena realised that she had given the game away. Undeterred she cut the operator off,

"I can't get through; I'll try their other number," she said, her voice panicked.

Miles' lunged forward stumbling. By a small margin, he avoided tripping over an armchair in his frantic advance.

Aunt Helena's fingers moved with urgency as she pressed the speed dial for the water taxi. The line connected a moment before Miles snatched it away from her grasp. In a desperate effort to disconnect, she reached for the button, but Miles' free hand barged her shoulder, thwarting her efforts.

"What have you done?" his angry shout echoed; his face twisted in fury.

A voice on the other end of the phone said, "Mount Clifford Water Taxis, how can I help you?"

"Nothing, I told you, I was trying to get through to the water taxis. Listen, they have answered now."

Aunt Helena could see the rage in Miles' eyes.

Beyond him, Lillie entered the room, her face pale with worry.

Miles turned to Lillie, his eyes bulging with anger, Aunt Helena used the distraction to push him to the ground. With a swift movement, she capitalised on the short window of opportunity, wasting no time as she leaped away from Miles.

"Run, Lillie!" Aunt Helena's voice rang out. Slicing like a dagger into the stress.

Lillie froze, her mind struggling to process the sudden turn of events.

In the meantime, Aunt Helena sprinted across the room, darting left and right between the furniture with a grace that belied the firebolt of pain in her shoulder.

Miles regained his footing, his gaze burning with determination.

Aunt Helena reached Lillie. She grabbed her niece's arm, sweeping her into the hall and slamming the door shut behind them. The impact shook the frame.

"Come on, we have to leave this place," Aunt Helena said. Her voice cracked with exhaustion, but her resolve remained unyielding.

"But where will we go?" Lillie said.

"We need to be away from him," Aunt Helena answered.

A thunderous growl erupted in the sky above the house. It served as a grim backdrop to their frantic escape.

Aunt Helena dragged Lillie by the wrist. They turned into an adjacent hallway; the urgency palpable in every step. However, their path to the front door was blocked by Miles, who approached from the other direction, having slipped out of the other lounge door.

"The kitchen," Aunt Helena said, panting, her mind racing for a way out.

"Yes, there's a backdoor there!" Lillie snapped back. Her instincts kicked in as she broke free from Aunt Helena's grasp.

"Come on, Aunt," she said.

Miles began closing in, his eyes burning. Their desperation grew. They dashed off, running the other way. Their breaths ragged and hearts raging in their chests.

The thunderous growl persisted overhead - a relentless symphony of dread amplifying their anxiety.

"There is Lillie, we can escape from there!" Aunt Helena said, between hurried breaths, as she followed Lillie.

They barrelled past stainless steel preparation tables. Adrenaline pushing them forward. Lillie pulled over one of the counters, blocking their pursuer's path.

They reached for the backdoor.

They found it locked. Panic surged through them. Miles's footsteps drew nearer. Aunt Helena's voice rose in urgency.

"No time to find a key! The stairs!" Aunt Helena urged, they pivoted, sprinting up the nearest flight.

The deafening roar continued, an ominous soundtrack to their frantic escape.

Every step they took was like a race against time, their heartbeats quickening in time with their thunderous steps.

Reaching Lillie's room, they slammed the door shut, their breaths coming in ragged gasps as they turned the key in the lock.

The room, for now, became a refuge, albeit a fragile one in the face of the unfolding chaos.

Through the window, flashes of light illuminated the darkened skies. It signalled the approach of an unknown threat. The unnerving growl persisted, vibrating through the building's walls.

They watched as the source of the deafening noise revealed itself. A police helicopter descending upon the lawn outside. Aunt Helena and Lillie shared astonished glances, as it dawned on them that aid had now arrived.

They huddled together in the corner of the room. Their hearts raced, as the aircraft landed with a reverberating thud. Its rotor blades cast blinking shadows through the window.

Outdoors, voices, muffled by the distance, reached their ears. A flurry of activity unfolding under the cover of the weather.

A ray of hope washed over the crushing uncertainty, as they saw flashing lights and the presence of the police.

Aunt Helena's hand shook as she tried to clutch Lillie's tighter. Their eyes fixed on the scene outside. The commotion now surreal.

Witnessing everything from the safety of their room, the tension began to dissipate. Substituted for a sense of guarded reassurance.

They waited, their breaths held in anticipation, as the authorities started to take control of things.

Aunt Helena and Lillie stayed in their room. They hunched

together. The anxious minutes dragged into an hour. They sat in silence.

Both debated whether to venture downstairs, to seek clarity about the ongoing situation. Yet, the continuing unease and uncertainty kept them planted in the security of their locked room.

"Why haven't the police come up here?" Lillie said. Her voice quivered with confusion as she peered out of the window, seeking answers.

Aunt Helena shook her head, her expression mirrored Lillie's disbelief.

"I'm not sure I get it," she said.

The sound of voices and sporadic commotion on the ground floor hinted at a sense of progress below, but the absence of direct contact from the authorities heightened their worry.

Their thoughts drifted back to Miles. His calculated demeanour created a lingering doubt over the unfolding events. Speculation brewed in their minds. They feared what he might be telling the investigators. It added another layer of concern to their already frayed nerves.

Aunt Helena gritted her teeth, her mind racing with countless unanswered questions.

"Should we go down there and see what's happening? It's been long enough," she said.

Lillie hesitated; her fear mingled with a growing curiosity.

"What if it's not safe?" she said.

In the middle of their deliberation, a knock struck the wooden door. Unexpected, it sent a jolt of surprise through both women. They exchanged a puzzled glance, wondering who would seek them out rather than summoning them downstairs.

A voice from the other side called out. "This is DI Bennetts. I need to ask you some questions."

Aunt Helena approached the door with caution. Her hand shook as she reached for the handle. She drew in a long breath and opened the door, revealing a police detective standing in the hallway.

DI Rosie Bennetts stood with an air of authority, her expression a blend of concern and professional.

"Thank you, you must be Helena?" she said.

"Yes." Aunt Helena replied, nervousness obvious in her voice.

"Helena, this is DC Archer. Would you go with him please so that I can have a chat with your companion," she said, thumbing through her notebook. "Lillie, isn't it?"

"Why are you separating us? We haven't done anything," Aunt Helena protested. "It's Miles Beaumont you should be talking to, he's the one that's been lying."

"Helena, it's just procedure," DI Bennetts said, in a firm but calm manner. "I have taken a statement from Mr Beaumont. I need to take one from everyone who was here last night, to establish the facts."

"Please, Helena, come with me. We will wait for DI Bennetts in your room," DC Archer said, holding his hand out in a gesture.

Helena sighed, looking back at Lillie as she went.

"Will you be, okay?" she said.

"Aunt Helena, I will be fine, I have nothing to hide." Lillie said, her voice confident despite her anxiety.

DI Bennetts stepped into the room.

"I'm here to speak with you about what happened earlier," she said.

"There are some matters we need to..." as her gaze settled on Lillie.

"You, Lillie," her eyes narrowed, curious at what she was seeing. "Sorry, I didn't make the connection. Now some of what I have heard makes sense."

Lillie turned towards the detective.

"The woman that tried to stop me and my son from getting on the bus," DC Bennetts said, observing with thoughtful contemplation, as though it held significance to the unfolding events.

Lillie flinched at the memory of the horrific crash.

Lowering her voice, she said. "How is he Rosie."

"Oh, he's fine, a little odd event like that can't shake him."

Lillie was perplexed; she thought the incident was more than a 'little odd'.

"Now, I have taken Mr Beaumont statement. He confirmed there is a body in the well. I can confirm that is true," she said. "I have an officer posted there now. He will protect any evidence. Mr Beaumont checked the CCTV. It shows the only person who left the house last night was you. So, in your own words. Can you tell me what happened?"

Lillie breathed in heavily, her thoughts running away, as she recounted the awful scene from the night before.

D.I. Bennett's stare gave nothing away. Lillie steadied herself and began.

"I went to bed and woke up near the well," she said. "It may have been either a nightmare or a premonition. I witnessed something dreadful. Something that was going to happen to Miles."

DI Bennetts raised an eyebrow, leaning forward, she said. "A premonition?"

"Yes," Lillie continued, recounting the traumatic occurrences that she had seen.

"Then I was back here. I was confused," she said, pausing. "Aunt Helena was here, sat with me. She told me it was a dream, a nightmare, but it was so vivid – I've had these visions before. I've tried but I don't understand them, they come true though."

The detective listened with intent, as Lillie detailed the other events of that night, explaining how she had warned Miles and the disbelief that had greeted her concerns.

"Aunt Helena didn't believe me at first, about the well," she said. "But after Miles claimed he checked and found nothing, she investigated herself and discovered the body in the well. Then she phoned the police for help straight away. We didn't believe Miles when he said he had done it."

DI Bennetts sat, her expression calm, contemplating what she was hearing. "So, according to your account, Aunt Helena confirmed your premonition, and she was the one who contacted us?"

"Yes, she went to the well and saw the body. You know she telephoned the emergency services. She was so brave," Lillie said, with a sense of hope that her viewpoint would now be taken with seriousness.

The detective shifted in her seat; her eyes narrowed to the notes she was making. "Thank you for your explaining everything, Lillie. Your story adds a new dimension to this."

Standing up, her face furrowed as she tried to piece together the information.

"Okay Lillie I am going to ask you to stay here for a bit, while I interview the other guests," she said, as she walked to the door and removed the key.

"Why are you taking that. Do you still suspect me?" she said, on the verge of tears.

"I don't know what to believe yet but there is a murderer on this island, so it is safer if I lock you in for the moment."

"One more thing, Lillie," she said as she opened the door. "Did you also have a premonition that day when we crossed paths on the mainland, and you attempted to block Sam and me from getting to the bus?"

"Yes. I have had a flood of visions over the last few weeks, or were they dreams? I don't know any more. I can never make sense of them. I was sure this time I could save Miles, but I got it wrong again, it wasn't even him. I thought I could save you and your son, but you wouldn't listen," Lillie said.

"I'm sorry I didn't believe you. What do you remember about the other visions or dreams?" she said.

She went on to tell DI Bennetts about the other visions she had been experiencing both on and before arriving at the island.

CHAPTER NINE

D I Bennetts swept past everyone in the room, her mere presence commanding attention. The room babbled with anticipation, guests shifting in their seats, apprehensive about what might happen.

With determined strides, she navigated through the assembled crowd, her stare sharp as she engaged each person one by one. The air hummed with tension as she questioned, studied, and then dismissed individuals as non-suspects.

The inquiry played out in the room, revealing a subtle balance of suspicion and relief.

"That leaves three people and whilst on the surface not everything adds up, their individual stories give us a clue to what may have happened."

"Miles and Helena, you were in the house all night until Lillie came back from the well. This raises questions about you, Lillie. You are the only one who had the opportunity," DI Bennetts stated, turning to Lillie with an accusatory stare. Lillie's terrified eyes grew wider. She averted her gaze from DI Bennetts, avoiding eye contact.

She continued. "However, Miles, you checked the well and reported there was nothing there. You have told me that you didn't want to cause distress to your guests, but the police were only called when Helena became suspicious and went to check herself, to find that indeed there was a body. You all have pieces to this puzzle, but none of them fit together."

Her eyes swept across the room; an investigator's scrutiny etched in every movement. A thoughtful glance landed on each face, seeking the subtlest hints of deceit - a furrowed brow, a nervous twitch, the fleeting tremor of uncertainty.

"Could it be that Miles is deceiving us and he managed to slip away in the night? Did he collude with Helena? Did Lillie concoct the vision as a ruse to hide her whereabouts?" she said

A weighted silence settled in the room, thickening with unspoken tension as DI Bennetts dissected the possibilities. Her words became a meticulous examination of the silent narratives etched in each person's expression.

DI Bennetts pondered the facts. The room waited, held in breathless anticipation. A sudden realisation hit her. Pausing mid-step, the pieces aligned in her mind, like an intricate mosaic. "Wait, Lillie, your vision. It wasn't an indication of anything to come at all, was it?"

Lillie frowned her brow at the detective's words, confused. "I don't understand."

"I recall, you told me that in your vision of the well, it was daylight, albeit dark from the storm," said DI Bennetts, her voice reverberated off the walls, carrying a revelation that shifted the feeling in the room. "Daylight? Yes, that changes everything."

Stopping, she turned back to the gathered guests, a conviction burning in her eyes. "When I met you on the mainland, you tried to stop my son and I get on a bus, why?"

Lillie shook her head, not understanding where this was going. "I've told you this. I had a premonition that the bus was going to crash, and your son was going to get hurt."

"Yes, but there was no collision with a bus. That discredits your story about having premonitions. However, there was one the week before where a child the same age as Sam was left with life changing injuries."

Lillie's eyes widened, a sudden hint of realisation.

"What if you are seeing visions of past events and not something about to happen. Yes, that has to be it," she said, punching the air with her fist.

"The codebreakers too, you saw them in a vision. A vision of something that happened years ago. I think it is called retrocognition," she continued.

"I don't understand," Lillie said.

"Lillie, I would put money on every vision you have ever had was an event from the past." Di Bennetts said. "If the vision you had last night were incidents that were not in the future, like the bus accident, which would open other lines of enquiry. The body in the well, the murder, it didn't happen last night, because in your vision it was daylight."

Her words lingered in the air. A heavy silence settled over the group. Their eyes betrayed a combination of fear and uncertainty, mirroring the unsettling tension that gripped the room.

The seconds ticked by. Not a single person dared to break the stillness.

"Lillie, you were also adamant that the man you witnessed being murdered was Miles Beaumont and yet here he is alive and well. I think, however, there is a truth in it, and you sir, she pointed to Miles Beaumont, are an imposter who most likely committed this evil act," she said." When forensics and backup arrive, we will soon find out for sure."

The oppressive hush persisted, each second dragging on until a voice shattered the suspense. Its tremor revealed the weight it carried.

DI Bennetts leaned forward, eyes glued to the man in front of her, as she probed for the facts.

"Okay, I'm not Miles," he said, his words strained and cracking under the pressure of hidden truths. The detective raised an eyebrow, urging the speaker to continue.

"I'm his brother, Tristram, I've been trapped here for years. It's not my fault," he said.

The man, they now knew as Tristam, avoided Bennetts' direct gaze, his eyes darted around the room. He continued. DI Bennetts recognised the uneasiness in his body language.

"They kept me locked away, and all I wanted was my life back. They called me mad, but he was the insane one," he said.

DI Bennetts exchanged a glance with DC Archer, a silent acknowledgment of the complexity of things. She gestured to Tristam to keep talking.

"He set me up, stole my life," Tristram said, his hands clenched into fists as he recounted the betrayal. Bennetts noticed his emotional turmoil, recognising the pain in the subtle quiver.

"Tell me everything," she urged, her tone both authoritative and empathetic. The room hung in suspense, waiting for the truth to unravel in the tense dialogue between detective and suspect.

Sibling, presumed dead by the outside world, wove a tale of thirty years shrouded in isolation on the remote island.

He described a life trapped in seclusion, hidden from the public. Everyone sat entranced, the facts lingering like a long-held secret.

In a tearful recollection, Tristram spoke of Miles, a brother who had tortured him for years.

"You don't understand what it was like living in his shadow," he said, his voice choked with emotion. "He did sadistic, twisted things. And I... I was the one who always got the blame."

DI Bennetts leaned forward, her expression encouraging him to continue. "Tell me, Tristram. What happened?"

Tristram turned to her, his eyes distant with the painful memory, "Years ago, Miles fell into the well. I was there. I saved him, hanging on to him while screaming for help. The gardener heard the screams and helped pull him free," he paused, a shudder running through him. "When we got home, he lied. He told mum and dad that I had pushed him."

DI Bennetts maintained her unwavering stare, urging him to share more.

In an outpouring, decades in the making, Tristram's voice broke as he spoke of the years of pain. "My parents bought people's silence. They were owners of all the local newspapers and were able to publish my obituary without anyone questioning them. Then they locked me up here because they thought I was insane."

Tristram continued speaking. The enormity of the revelation rocked the room. DI Bennetts absorbed the details, remaining silent an invitation for him to reveal the depths of the injustice he had endured.

"When Miles came to the island, he discovered me. We argued. I wanted my life back. Then he ran. I panicked went after him. Then when he tripped, I saw my opportunity to stop him," he said, his explanation racing out. "No body had really seen him in public for years. We have such similar appearances. I thought I could pass myself off as him. Get my life back, I did for a while."

DI Bennetts' words pierced through the tension. "DC Archer, cuff him and read him his rights."

Tristram was arrested on suspicion of murder, the tense mood in the house dissolved again into a sombre stillness.

DI Bennetts, with a decisive nod, signalled DC Archer to proceed. The clicking of handcuffs filled the room as they restrained him and escorted him away.

Outside, the storm had calmed, leaving a dark silence that matched the general feel of the guests.

DI Bennetts addressed the guests: "You are welcome to stay but many parts of the house and the island are now a crime scene, so movement will be restricted. If you wish to leave, please make sure your contact details are left with myself or DC. Archer, as we may need to be in touch with you, to ask you further questions."

Lillie's eyes pleaded as she glared at her aunt. Aunt Helena spoke, concern obvious in her voice. "DI Bennetts, Lillie and I came here for some respite, you can see that has not been the case. She simply wants to go home, to find some peace."

"Of course, I will take your contact information and then you are free to go."

DI. Bennetts led Lillie and Aunt Helena to the jetty later that day. Her face reflecting a thoughtful contemplation. They strolled along the path, exchanging small talk, delving into the events that had unravelled on the secluded island.

The sea breeze whipped strands of their hair back, as the constant reassurance of waves lapping the sands provided a backdrop to their conversation.

"I understand now. Those visions... they were not of the future. In the first premonition I ever had, I thought I had seen my sister drowning before it happened, but it was a vision of a past event, something I couldn't have changed. Now I know that I could never have saved her," Lillie said.

Looking away, she watched the mist as it rolled in closer from the horizon.

DI Bennetts paused, glancing at Lillie with understanding. "I get it. It must have been an awful burden."

DI Bennetts was lost in thought, considering Lillie's revelation. "Sometimes, those sorts of visions can be just as significant. Perhaps, someday, your gift could aid us in solving some cases. People disappear all the time. You might be able to find them."

Reaching the jetty, Lillie viewed the fog that still hung like a menacing dog off the shoreline.

She listened but all she heard where the sounds of the water. It was as though the mysterious whispers that had plagued her for so long, had at last found their silence, following the discovery of the truth.

She turned to DI Bennetts, her eyes reflecting a newfound sense of closure and uttered, with a mixture of relief and contemplation in her voice.

"The whispers in the fog, they've stopped."

Printed in Great Britain
by Amazon